The ★ Snowchild

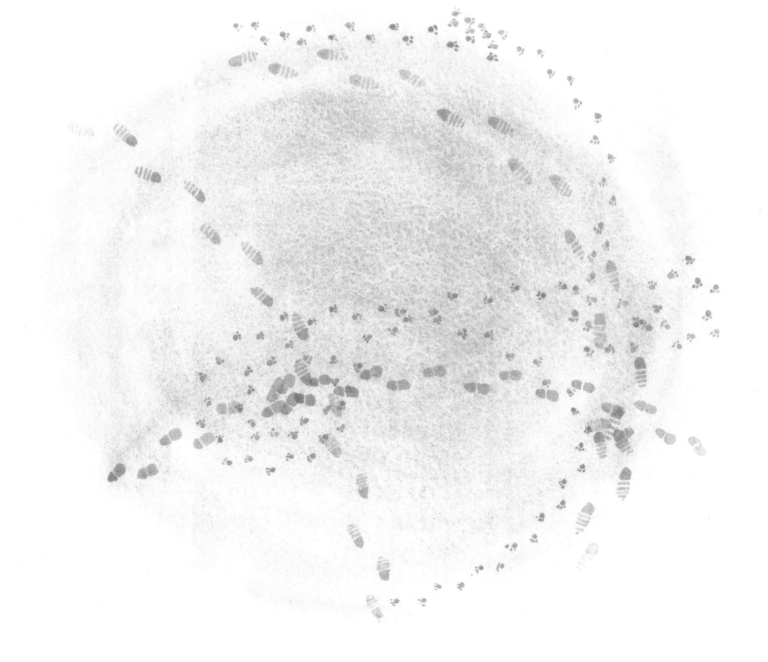

To Jesse with love

★

ISBN 0-439-24243-6

The Snowchild copyright © 1994 by Frances Lincoln Limited.
Text and illustrations copyright © 1994 by Debi Gliori.
All rights reserved.
Published by Scholastic Inc., 555 Broadway, New York, NY 10012,
by arrangement with Simon & Schuster Books for Young Readers,
Simon & Schuster Children's Publishing Division.
SCHOLASTIC and associated logos are trademarks and/or registered
trademarks of Scholastic Inc.

12 11 10 9 8 7 6 5 4 3 2 1   0 1 2 3 4 5/0

Printed in the U.S.A.   14

First Scholastic printing, December 2000

The Snowchild

Debi Gliori

SCHOLASTIC INC.
New York Toronto London Auckland Sydney
Mexico City New Delhi Hong Kong

In the last of the light before nighttime,
children come to play games in the park.
They play in groups, they play in pairs,
together in a circle, to keep the night away.

Standing on the sidelines, there
was a small girl called Katie.
Katie-left-out.
Katie-who-didn't-know-how-to-play.
She had ideas for lots of good games, but
somehow never played them at the right time.

In the early spring, when afternoon
rain left the streets shiny-bright,
Katie appeared with
a newspaper boat.

"Let's sail this in a puddle,"
she said.

The other children stared at her.

"But we're playing shipwrecks,"
said Ruth, stamping so hard
that a muddy wave sank Katie's boat.
    Everyone ran off,
jumping and splashing,
trying to soak one another.

Katie walked home alone.

By summer the streets were dusty
and tired. Everyone played
in the leafy shade by the pond
in the park.

Katie arrived with a basket and began to
fill it with pebbles.

"Let's play shipwrecks," she said.

The other children looked at her in dismay.

"But we're playing piggy-in-the-middle," said Tim.
He grabbed Katie's basket, tipping out
the pebbles, and threw it in the water.
The basket floated away across the pond.

Katie fished out her basket
and walked home alone.

Autumn came, and the trees in the park turned gold.
The children played there, scattering leaves as they ran.

When Katie saw all the children, she picked up a ball
that was rolling on the fallen leaves.

"Let's play piggy-in-the-middle," she said.

Bennet's baby brother Nick burst into tears.

"Give that ball back to my little brother!" yelled Bennet.

Katie dropped the ball and ran home crying. All she wanted was to join in. All she wanted was to be part of the circle.

Winter came, and Katie
was lonelier than ever.
It was too cold to play
outside, and no one
invited Katie over
to play.

One morning Katie woke up early,
and at once she knew that something
had changed. Bright light was shining
into her bedroom, and it was quiet
and still outside.

When Katie looked out her window,
she saw that the city was covered with snow,
deep, white snow.

Katie knew exactly what to do.
She put on her warmest clothes
and ran to the park.

There she heard the sound of
children playing.

She saw Bennet
whizzing down
a slope on his sled.

She saw Tim
wobbling downhill
on his skis.

She saw Ruth making snow angels
by the pond.

Katie sighed a little
and walked on until she
found an untouched
patch of perfect snow,
and there she started
to make a snowman.

She made a little snowball, and
then she patted on more snow
until it was big enough to roll on
the ground, round and round,
till the snowball
came up to
her tummy.
That was the
snowman's body.

Then Katie made a smaller
ball for the snowman's head.
She carefully lifted the head
onto the body and stood back
to admire it.

The snowman was very
small, not really as big
as a man at all.

"I know what you are," said Katie.
"You're a snowchild! But poor you,
you haven't any eyes
or even a smile, and
you must be frozen
without a hat. Wait here,
and I'll run home and find
some things for you."

Katie rushed home and started to fill a basket
for her snowchild. He'll need these, she thought,
picking up some coal in the garden shed—and
a carrot from the kitchen, too.

She found a hat under Mom
and Dad's bed and a very warm scarf
on the chair in her bedroom.
Then she rushed outside again.

She ran and ran, past Bennet, past Tim, past Ruth, until, at last . . .

Katie stopped in surprise.

There, beside her snowchild, was a snowman.

It didn't have any eyes or a smile, either.

Poor thing, thought Katie, once I've finished my snowchild, I'll run home for some bits for you.

She put her basket down and unpacked it. First the eyes and nose. Then Katie drew a smile with her finger.

Next she put a woolly hat on the snowchild's head and tenderly wrapped a scarf around his neck. Last of all, she patted the snowchild, and he seemed to smile back.

"What a brilliant snowman," said a voice.

Katie looked around and saw a small girl carrying a bag.

"Look, I've brought some yarn to make hair for mine,"
she said. "I'm going to call her Jenny, like me.
What's yours called?"

"I'm calling him Snowchild
because he's so small," said Katie.

"When I finish this one," said Jenny,
"let's make another one—together."
   Katie's smile grew wider than her snowchild's.
"A snowdad," Katie said, laughing.
   "And a snowmom," added Jenny.
   "With some snowfriends," said Katie.
   "Just like us," said Jenny.

By the time darkness fell,
the park was full of friends:
snowfriends, snowchildren,
real friends, and real
children who played
and laughed and
rolled in the snow.

And Katie wasn't watching
from the sidelines.
She was there in the circle,
playing with her new friend.